Pinocchio Meets the Cat and Fox

By Carlo Collodi
Adapted by David E. Cutts

Illustrated by Diane Paterson

TROLL ASSOCIATES

Library of Congress Cataloging in Publication Data

Cutts, David.
    Pinocchio meets the cat and fox.

    (The Adventures of Pinocchio library; 2)
    Summary: Pinocchio is tricked into planting his gold
coins in the Field of Miracles by the evil Cat and Fox.
    [1. Fairy tales. 2. Puppets and puppet-plays—
Fiction] I. Collodi, Carlo, 1826-1890. II. Paterson,
Diane, 1946-   ill. III. Collodi, Carlo, 1826-1890.
Pinocchio. IV. Title. V. Series.
PZ8.C96Pi   [Fic]   81-16427
ISBN 0-89375-716-0 (case)   AACR2
IBSN 0-89375-717-9 (pbk.)

Printed in the United States of America
10 9 8 7 6 5 4 3 2 1

Pinocchio was on his way home. All night, he had been held a prisoner by the Puppet Master, the man who ran the puppet show that Pinocchio had gone to see. But now Pinocchio was free, and he had made up his mind to be good from now on. In his pocket were the five gold coins the Puppet Master had given him. Now Pinocchio could buy a new coat for Geppetto and a new spelling book for himself. But first, he would go straight home to Geppetto's house.

He had not gone far when he met a lame Fox and a blind Cat.
"Ah, Pinocchio! We know your poor father quite well," the
Fox said. "Quite well," repeated the Cat. "My father is not
poor any more," announced Pinocchio, holding up the five
gold coins. The Fox flashed a greedy smile and said, "Why not
come with us, and make your money grow?"

Pinocchio thought he heard a voice whisper, "Don't listen to them." So he said, "I must go straight home. But first, tell me how my money can grow." The Fox smiled. "If you plant your coins in the Field of Miracles, they will grow into money trees," said the Fox. "Money trees," repeated the Cat. Pinocchio liked that idea. So without another thought, he set off with the Fox and the Cat.

They walked and they walked, and when evening came, they arrived at an inn. They went inside, where the Fox and the Cat ordered the best foods, and ate until they could eat no more. Pinocchio hardly ate at all, for he could think of nothing but the Field of Miracles. Then the Fox suggested that they sleep for a few hours, and continue their journey at midnight.

At midnight, Pinocchio woke up and looked around. "Where
are the Fox and the Cat?" he asked. The innkeeper replied,
"Your companions have gone ahead, and will wait for you at
the Field of Miracles. They said that you would gladly pay for
their dinners." So Pinocchio gave the innkeeper one of his gold
coins, and left the inn.

The night was dark and still. As Pinocchio walked alone, he heard a voice. "Turn back, Pinocchio," said the voice. "Do not trust those who promise to make you rich in a day." It was the Talking Cricket. But Pinocchio replied, "I have made up my mind to go on." The Cricket said, "Boys who must have their own way are often sorry later." Then he disappeared.

Pinocchio was left alone. He began talking to himself. "Everyone tells me what to do," he said. "And when I make up my own mind, they tell me I will be sorry." Suddenly, he heard a noise behind him. Not too far away were two evil-looking figures wearing sacks to hide their faces. Pinocchio did not notice that these two strangers were exactly the same size as the Fox and the Cat.

"Robbers!" thought Pinocchio. "I must hide my money."
But he could think of no place to hide his coins. So when the
robbers came closer, he popped the coins into his mouth. Then
he tried to run, but the robbers grabbed him by the arm. "Give
us your money or your life," said the first. "Or your life,"
repeated the second.

10

Pinocchio pretended he had no money. But the first robber said, "Where did you hide the gold coins?" "Gold coins," repeated the second. Pinocchio was so scared that he trembled. The gold coins began to clink. *"Aha!"* said the robbers. "Open your mouth." But Pinocchio would not do it. He began to struggle. He kicked and he scratched and he fought.

Finally, Pinocchio got away. He jumped over a hedge and ran until he could run no more. Then he tried to hide in a tree. But the robbers found him, and built a fire under the tree. Soon it was so hot that Pinocchio could not stand it any longer. He jumped from the tree and raced across the open fields.

By the time the sun came up, Pinocchio had come to a wide ditch that was filled with dirty water. He jumped across it before the robbers could catch him. Now the robbers had to jump across the ditch. But since they were wearing sacks, they could not jump far enough. *Splash! Splash!* A few minutes later, two wet robbers were again chasing Pinocchio.

Pinocchio ran and ran until he could run no farther. The robbers were coming closer! The first robber reached out and seized Pinocchio by the collar. "You won't get away from us this time," he cried. "This time," repeated the other. Then they tried to force Pinocchio to open his mouth so they could take the gold coins.

It was no use. Pinocchio would not open his mouth. "We must hang him!" the first robber said. "Hang him!" repeated the second. And so they hung Pinocchio from a branch of the big oak tree, and waited for his jaw to drop open. Soon they grew tired of waiting, and said, "We will come back tomorrow. By then, the puppet should be ready to open his mouth."

As soon as the robbers went away, a terrible storm began. The wind blew Pinocchio back and forth, and the rope seemed to get tighter and tighter. He was sure he was dying. Finally, his eyes closed, and his whole body went limp. Lucky for Pinocchio, the Good Fairy happened to live nearby. She cut Pinocchio down from the tree and brought him to her house.

Three doctors examined Pinocchio. Dr. Crow said, "If that puppet is not dead, then he may still be alive." Dr. Owl said, "If he is not alive, then he must be dead." The third doctor was really the Talking Cricket. He said, "That puppet is a disobedient son who will break his father's heart!" Then, as the doctors left the room, the Fairy heard someone crying softly. It was Pinocchio!

17

The Fairy brought out some medicine and said, "Drink this, and you will feel better. It will taste bitter, but I will give you a lump of sugar with it." Pinocchio took the sugar, but he refused to drink the medicine. The Fairy warned, "Unless you take your medicine, you will surely die." Still, Pinocchio would not drink it.

Suddenly, the door flew open, and four rabbits came in, carrying a coffin. "We have come for Pinocchio," they said. Pinocchio cried out, "But I am not dead yet!" The rabbits replied, "Without your medicine, you have only a few minutes left." At once, Pinocchio took the medicine from the Fairy, and drank it down. Then the rabbits turned and left as quickly as they had come.

Soon Pinocchio was as good as new. He told the Fairy everything that had happened to him. "And where are the gold coins now?" the Fairy asked. Pinocchio had them in his pocket, but he replied, "I lost them!" As soon as he told this lie, his nose grew longer. "Where did you lose them?" asked the Fairy. "In the woods," replied Pinocchio. And his nose grew longer still.

"We must go and look for them," said the Fairy. Suddenly, Pinocchio cried out, "Wait! I remember now! I swallowed the coins!" With this third lie, Pinocchio's nose grew so long that he could not turn around without bumping into the walls. The Fairy began to laugh. But Pinocchio could do nothing except sit down and cry.

The Fairy wanted to teach Pinocchio a lesson about lying, so she let him keep his long nose for a while. Finally, she clapped her hands, and some woodpeckers flew in through the open window. They perched on Pinocchio's nose and started pecking away at it. Before long, the nose was back to its usual size.

Pinocchio thanked the Fairy for all she had done. Then he said, "Now I must return home to my father." The Fairy replied, "Geppetto knows where you are, and he will be here tonight." But Pinocchio cried, "I cannot wait that long to see him. I will leave now, and meet him on the road." And so Pinocchio waved good-by and started off to meet his father.

As he passed the big oak tree, he came upon the Fox and the Cat. "Greetings!" said the Fox. "How is it that you happen to be here?" Pinocchio told them everything that had happened. "After I left the inn, two robbers attacked me," he said. "Fortunately, they did not get my money. Now I am going to meet Geppetto, and give him the gold coins."

The Fox sighed, "To think that instead of only four coins, you could give him thousands. Just come with us to the Field of Miracles." "Miracles," repeated the Cat. But Pinocchio replied, "Perhaps tomorrow." Then the Fox said, "Tomorrow will be too late. After today, no one will be allowed to plant their money." So, again, Pinocchio went off with the Fox and the Cat.

When they finally reached the Field of Miracles, it looked like any other field. The Fox said, "Dig a hole, and drop your coins in. Cover the coins with dirt, and then water them." Pinocchio followed the instructions exactly. "Now we must go," said the Fox. "If you return in twenty minutes, you will find a tree that is covered with money." Then they all went away.

When the twenty minutes had passed, Pinocchio started back toward the Field of Miracles. He thought of what he would do with all the money that would be growing on the trees. But when he arrived at the field, he saw nothing. Nothing was growing where he had planted his coins. "Something must have gone wrong!" he cried.

Suddenly, a parrot in a nearby tree began laughing. "Are you laughing at *me*?" asked Pinocchio. The parrot replied, "I am laughing at anyone who believes money grows on trees. The only way to get money is to earn it—unless you are like the Fox and the Cat. While you were gone, they returned and dug up your gold coins. Now they have run away."

Pinocchio could hardly believe his ears. He began digging in the very place where he had buried his money. Deeper and deeper he dug, but he found nothing except rocks and dirt. At last, he realized that the parrot had spoken the truth. The Fox and the Cat had run off with his money. He had been robbed!

Right next to the Field of Miracles was the Village of Blockheads. Pinocchio ran to the Village Court and reported the robbery. The judge was a gorilla who was so old that he could not see very well. He listened patiently as Pinocchio told his story. Then, when Pinocchio had finished, the judge reached out and rang a bell.

Two dogs in police uniforms appeared. The judge pointed to Pinocchio and said, "Two robbers have taken the puppet's money. Throw him in jail!" Poor Pinocchio! The police dogs dragged him away, and no one would listen to his cries. He was locked in a prison cell, and there he stayed for four months.

At last, a lucky thing happened. Everyone who had been thrown into jail in the Village of Blockheads was set free. So Pinocchio left the village, and headed down the road. From now on, he would do as he was told. From now on, he would behave so well that Geppetto would be proud of him. And so, older and wiser, Pinocchio headed home at last.